DIS

MYSTERY IN THE PIRATE OAK

Mystery in the Pirate Oak

BY HELEN FULLER ORTON

Illustrated by Robert Doremus

J. B. LIPPINCOTT COMPANY
PHILADELPHIA AND NEW YORK

Tenth Printing

Library of Congress catalog card number 49-9989

CONTENTS

MYSTERY IN THE PIRATE OAK

1. The Old Oak

CHAD TURNER pushed open the screen door and went through to the porch with his stamp collection in his arms.

He had two large stamp albums, both partly filled, and a catalog he had just bought. In his right hand he carried a package of letters Mother had found when she was cleaning the attic.

"You may find some interesting stamps on some of these old covers," she had said as she handed them to him.

Chad went to a table at one end of the porch and sat down to his work of comparing the stamps on the envelopes with the pages of the catalog. Every little while he gave a whistle, as he discovered a stamp on one of the covers to fill a vacant place in one of the albums. "Say! This is quite a find!" he would exclaim.

These letters were very old, dated not long after postage stamps were first issued. He picked up one envelope after another, putting in a pile by themselves those that he knew were the most valuable.

"Gee!" he exclaimed, when he came to one with the date 1860 on the postmark, "This is quite a find! Now if I could only find one that was issued in 1847! Or, even one dated earlier than that! If only I could find a postmaster stamp ! That would be grand! But I guess I'll never get one of those."

"How do you know?" his sister Ellie asked. "You might."

She had come out on the porch so quietly that Chad didn't realize she was there until she spoke.

"I probably never will. They *are* awful scarce," he sighed.

"I don't see why you care so much for those stamps," Ellie said, with a toss of her head. "I'd a lot rather read a good story than to fuss with little pieces of paper with pictures on them."

"It's fun," Chad returned. "These are not just pictures. They mean something. And some day I might find one that is very scarce and worth a lot of money."

After looking through the bundle of envelopes and finding nothing earlier than 1860, Chad cut that one from the cover and dropped it into a saucer of water to soak it off the paper.

Chad wasn't his real name. When he wrote his name in school, it was Charles. And Ellie's was Elaine. Their father had died a few years before. The house he and Ellie and their mother lived in was about a mile outside the village.

There were only two houses near their home. The road ran east and west. Beyond them to the west, on the same side of the road there was a fine large house that had been vacant two years. It was called the Peterson place. Between the two houses there was a meadow.

Across the road from their house was another vacant house, a small one. It wasn't exactly across, but a little way to the west. In fact, it stood just opposite the middle of the meadow. That house was called the old Whitman place. Never since Chad and Ellie could remember had anyone lived there. It was an old gray house, not very large, but it had a homey, comfortable look.

"I do wish people would move into one of these houses," Mother sometimes said. "It would be nice to have neighbors and to see lights in those windows in the evening."

Their own house, though not very large, was a pleasant one and sturdily built. Chad and Ellie liked it, partly because they had always lived there, partly because it had many windows and the sunshine was allowed to come in and make the place bright and cheery.

Also, they liked to live there because there was a noble old oak tree in the meadow and they had good times playing in it.

It was a hot day in the middle of August. When Chad finished with his stamps for that day, he put the albums and catalog and the old letters away in a safe place.

He got a drink of cold water from the ice box and a cooky from the cooky jar, then ran out to the porch again.

"Ellie, let's go over to the old oak," he said. "Maybe it's cooler there."

"All right."

"It's a good idea," Mother remarked. "If I were your age, I'd go there myself. And I don't mind your climbing it, since there is grassy ground underneath it. If we lived in the city, I wouldn't want you to climb the trees along the streets, for if you should fall, you might be hurt by the hard pavement."

"Do come with us," Ellie urged. "You could sit in the shade under the tree and rest."

"I'd love to, but I have many things to do," Mother told them.

Mother was a school teacher. It was nice to have her at home these vacation days, for all the rest of the year she had to leave early and be gone all day.

"I wish we had a car," Chad said. "Then we could go down to the beach and go in swimming on a day like this."

They lived on Long Island. The Atlantic Ocean was only a few miles away, but it was a long walk to the beach.

"Why not wish for the moon and a dozen stars?" teased Ellie. "You know we can't have a car. We can't have any new things except those we need badly."

She was sorry as soon as the words were out of her mouth, for she noticed the sad look on Mother's face.

"You could drive it if we had one, couldn't you,

Mom?" Chad asked.

"Oh, yes. I've driven many thousands of miles. I love to drive. But I think we'll just have to do without a car until you children are through school. I can't possibly manage to get one now."

Chad wasn't one to make a fuss if a thing couldn't be helped. "Come on, Sis," he called. "Let's go over to the old oak."

He scooted out the side door, through a break in the hedge and across the grassy meadow to the big oak tree in the middle of it.

They always called it the old oak. It was a beautiful tree, with many branches that spread out in all directions. Not long before he died, their father had built a little house in the old tree for them to play in. It was only a platform built among the branches, with no roof and no walls, but they called it the tree house.

When Ellie reached the old oak, Chad had already scrambled up the trunk to the tree house. He was sitting on the floor, his feet hanging over the edge.

Ellie climbed up the rough trunk, stepping on little humps and holding on to little twigs. A few feet from the ground the trunk divided into two limbs, making it not too hard to climb.

"I'll bet this tree is a hundred years old," Chad said, as he watched Ellie clamber up.

"Why, Chad, it's much older than a hundred. I'll bet it's two hundred years old. It's an oak tree. Oaks grow slowly and live long. I learned that in Nature Study."

"Might be," Chad agreed. Ellie was two years younger, but she had read more books. She was nine and would go into the fourth grade in the fall.

Chad frequently let her have her own way when they differed, but now he said, "It couldn't be two hundred. Just think of all the big storms that have raged here. A tree two hundred years old would have blown down in one of them."

"Not an oak tree," Ellie contended. "It's roots go down deep. It may bend before the wind, but it doesn't blow down."

"Have it your way," said Chad. "It's a nice old tree anyway." Ellie kept climbing till she reached the tree house. She sat on the floor of it, reached into a hollow in one of the big limbs at the side of it and took out a little tin box in which she kept candy bars and marshmallows.

"Would you like a marshmallow?" she asked. She held out the box for him to help himself, which he did.

"A big tree is an awful nice thing," said Chad, as he looked up among the high branches. "I'll bet there's a squirrel's nest up there somewhere. See the squirrel running along that limb above me?"

The little creature would run fast along a limb, jump to another one, then stand still and look down at them with its bright black eyes. It was a beautiful gray squirrel with a long bushy tail. As long as they kept perfectly still, he would stay there, frisking his tail, chattering fast. But the moment one of them moved he ran up the limb, jumped to another one and disappeared in some hollow.

"Where did he go?" Ellie asked.

"I'll climb up and find out where his hole is," Chad said. He stepped onto a big limb, then swung onto another one higher up.

"Be careful!" Ellie warned.

"Shucks! I never fell out of a tree yet," Chad bragged. "And I bet I've climbed this one a hundred times. And if I should fall, there's soft earth under the tree."

While he was hunting for the squirrel's nest, Ellie was watching a bird that had lighted on a twig not far away. It didn't seem to mind her being so near, but twittered and hopped along the limb, stopped and twittered again, hopped along, flew over to another twig and stood there chirping and fluttering its wings, as if saying, "I like to have you in my tree."

"A tree would be a fine place to live in on hot days," Ellie said.

From the tree they could see out only here and there between the leaves; but they could hear all sorts of sounds. A train was speeding along on the railroad a mile away. Crickets were chirping among the grass. Cars were speeding along the road. Overhead, an airplane was flying toward the nearby airport.

"I'll bet a lot of birds have their nests here," Ellie said. "A lot of squirrels too. Is there any other kind of creature that lives in an oak tree?"

"Worms and bugs. And every year an oriole makes its nest away out at the end of that limb near the top. Say, Ellie, I'll bet if this old tree could talk, it would have a lot of interesting things to tell."

"Maybe it has a lot of secrets," Ellie said, as she noticed a little hollow place partly grown over with bark.

Chad kept climbing higher till he was far above Ellie. He liked to climb high. But Ellie liked to stay in the tree house. After a while she called up, "Come on down, Chad. Let's play Chinese checkers."

He came down cheerfully enough, for it was his favorite game, and for another hour they stayed in the tree playing with the checker board on the floor of the play house, birds chirping around them, airplanes flying overhead.

"This is a nice game for a hot day," said Ellie, as she jumped her last marble into place. "It makes us forget the weather is hot."

When Mother called them to lunch, they slid down and were starting off across the meadow toward home when Ellie suddenly said, "Look, Chad! There's a man going into the Peterson house! I wonder if someone is going to move in there."

They stopped and looked toward the big house beyond the meadow——the house that had been empty for two years.

"Might be," said Chad.

"I hope they are nice folks," said Ellie.

Again they heard Mother calling, "Chad! Ellie!"

They walked off toward home on slow unwilling feet.

Their white cat, Frosty, came to meet them. Ellie stooped to stroke her neck. "You should have been with us," she said. "You love it in that tree."

The three went along together, Frosty ahead, till they had gone through the break in the hedge. Then Frosty went to her favorite place on the grass under the apple tree in the back yard. Chad and Ellie went into the dining room for lunch.

2. *Grandmother Hale*

THE NEXT forenoon Chad came running into the house,
all excited. "Oh, Mother, there is a moving van in
front of the old Whitman place!"

"Can it be possible that someone is moving in there?"
said Mother, coming to the front door.

Chad and Ellie ran across the road and watched the moving men carrying furniture into the house. It was not a very large house. Part of it, at the back, was the log house from which the Whitman family had moved, long ago, when they went west.

A new part had been built in front, so it looked like a modern house, only it had grown gray and needed painting.

They looked at the sign on the moving van. "Why, it's from Kansas!" Ellie exclaimed. "How exciting! Someone coming here from Kansas!"

"Who is coming to live here?" Chad asked one of the moving men.

"I don't know the name. One is an elderly lady. Maybe she is going to live here all alone. I don't know."

They ran home with the news. "It will be nice to see lights in the windows there," Mother said eagerly. "Such a long time that house has been empty and looked forlorn and lonely."

"Why is it called the Whitman place?" Ellie asked.

"It belonged to a pioneer family named Whitman. When they moved west, one of the brothers stayed here. When he went west, someone of another name lived there for a long time, but it has always kept the name of Whitman. I wonder if one of them is coming back."

"Hurrah! I hope there's a boy in the family to play with me," said Chad.

"I hope there's a girl," said Ellie.

"Humph!" said Chad. "Don't we have fun together in the old oak?"

"Oh, yes, of course. But sometimes I'd like to have a girl friend to talk to and play with."

Mrs. Turner was wondering what the new neighbors would be like. "I hope they'll clear up the yard. I'd like to see the shrubs trimmed and the grounds made tidy," was her thought.

The men finished carrying the furniture in and drove off.

"It's queer that they'd put furniture in and no one there to look after it," Ellie said.

Chad ran over and stepped inside the front door, which had been left open. The furniture was standing about, but no one was in sight. He called but no one answered.

"We'll keep an eye on it," Mother said, when Chad came back.

Every little while Mother glanced over at the old house to see that all was right. An hour later a car drove up and stopped. A young man got out, then helped an elderly lady.

"There they are! Two people for our new neighbors!" Chad called to Mother, who was in the back yard picking flowers.

She came into the house and looked across at the two people going up the walk. The lady was walking fast, as if she were glad to come to the place. The young man followed her, carrying two big satchels.

"Maybe it's her grandson," said Mother. "They look like nice folks and as if we'd like them for neighbors."

The young man went back and forth carrying all sorts of bundles they had brought in the car. All the afternoon the Turner family could get glimpses of him, putting big pieces of furniture in place, and of the lady putting dishes and books and other small things where they were to be kept.

Chad soon tired of seeing other folks doing things. He said, "Let's go over to the old oak. It's no fun watching folks settling their house." So he and Ellie ran over to the big tree.

Mother said to herself, "I'll go over and call on the new people right now. Maybe there is something I can do to help. And I'll take them a fresh apple pie." She had made two that morning.

That is how it happened that when Chad and Ellie

came in for supper, Mother told them, "I've found out who our new neighbor is to be."

Ellie looked up in astonishment. "But Mother, there are two of them," she said.

Mother smiled. "Yes, there are two of them now, but one is going back to Kansas."

"Which one?" Chad asked.

"The young man, the lady's grandson. Would you believe it? She is going to live there all alone."

"That is queer," said Ellie. "I should think she'd want someone with her."

"She would like someone, but there is no one who can come. She says she'll get on all right alone. And I believe it. She's that sort. We are going to like her for a neighbor. She's friendly and charming and altogether a likable person. After she is settled, she wants you two to go over to see her."

"What is her name?" Ellie asked.

"Mrs. Hale. But she says she is usually called Grandmother Hale. She is one of the old family who used to live in that house."

"But Mother, that family was named Whitman," said Chad.

"To be sure. And her name was Mary Whitman. Mrs. Hale is her married name."

"But she isn't really our grandmother," Ellie protested.

"No; but she likes to be called that."

"Suits me," said Chad, " 'specially as we haven't any grandmother living near."

In three days the young man had cleaned up the yard and trimmed some of the shrubs and was ready to go back to Kansas. He came over that day. "I'm glad to know that Grandmother is to have good neighbors," he told Mrs. Turner. "She is rather set in her ways. She insists on living here alone in the old house. I'd like it if you folks would go over to see her often."

"We'll be glad to," Mother assured him.

The next day, soon after he saw the young man start off to Kansas, Chad went over. When he went up the walk, Grandmother Hale was sitting on her porch.

"Good afternoon, Chad," she said in welcome.

"Good afternoon!" Chad replied. "How did you know my name?"

"Maybe one of the little birds flying around here told me," was her answer.

"Oh-h!" said Chad.

"I said 'Maybe.' As a matter of fact, my grandson found it out. He found out that you can climb trees too."

"Of course I can climb trees," Chad declared heartily.

"Maybe you can climb that big tree over there in the meadow."

"Oh, yes. I can do that. It is a good tree for climbing."

"I know that," she said. "I used to climb it myself when I was your age."

"Gee!" was all Chad could manage to say.

Grandmother Hale had a pleasant voice and she was good to look at, with her white hair and her blue eyes. Chad liked to talk with her, but he wondered a bit why she was so interested in his climbing trees.

He looked around for something to talk about. "There are lots of weeds in your yard," he said.

"Yes, I know it. My grandson pulled a good many, but not all. I must find someone to pull them. This is a nice place to live, if only it could be fixed up a bit. It needs a new roof and new paper on the walls and new front steps."

Chad glanced down at the steps, which surely did look old and worn.

Grandmother Hale went on, "Now if only I had the silver box, perhaps I could have a new roof put on the house and new paper on the walls and all the other things I need. But you can climb the old oak for me. I wanted my grandson to do it, but he wouldn't venture. He said it was silly to expect the silver box would be

there after all these years had passed; said he wasn't
going to risk his neck by climbing an old tree whose
limbs might break easily. He said there wasn't a chance
in a million that the box was still there."

"Why could you have a new roof if I should climb the
tree for you?" Chad asked. "What is up there?"

"The silver box—a little silver box with letters en-
graved on the cover. It was about this big." She showed
with her hands about five inches long and three inches
wide. "My grandfather, who was a sea captain, brought
it to me long ago from far away in the East, when he
came home from a long voyage."

"How did it come to be up in the big oak?" Chad
wanted to know.

"Come and sit here on the porch and I'll tell you."

Chad came up the rickety steps and took his seat on
the edge of the porch with his feet hanging over.

Grandmother Hale began: "Long ago, when I was a
little girl, we lived in this house. That big oak tree in
the meadow across the road was much smaller than it is
now. My brother and I used to climb it and have fun in
it, just as you and your sister do now. It was a good tree
for climbing then."

"And it is a good one still," Chad interrupted.

"Good! Well, as I was telling you, I climbed it the
very morning we were going to start west. Father and

Mother had decided that we would go west to the prairie country. Everything was packed in the big lumber wagon and they were doing the last things when I went over to climb the big tree for the last time. I had the silver box in my pocket."

"Oh, I can guess what happened," Chad exclaimed. "You dropped it on the ground and it broke."

"Wrong, my lad. I didn't drop it. And it couldn't break anyway, for it was made of silver. We girls had pockets in our dresses in those days. The silver box was in my pocket. As I climbed about, it would bother me by hitting against the branches, so I took it out of the pocket and put it in a hollow in the side of a limb."

"In a squirrel's nest?"

"No, just a hollow place. Then I climbed higher and sat on a limb and looked around through the big tree and felt lonesome to be leaving it. All of a sudden Father called me to come, saying they were ready to start and for me to hurry. I was so excited that I forgot about the silver box. I slid down the trunk of the tree and ran to the wagon, climbed up beside Mother and we started off."

"And you never saw the box again," Chad ventured.

"Never again. That day we rode on and on. And there were so many interesting things to see that I never once thought of the silver box."

"That was too bad," said Chad. "When did you remember it?"

"The next day, when we were many miles from home, I suddenly thought of it and put my hand in my pocket. I called out, 'We'll have to turn back, for I've left the silver box back in the old oak.' "

" 'We can't turn back,' Father said. 'We've gone a whole day's journey over rough roads. We mustn't turn back, no matter what was left behind.' "

"Then what did you do?" Chad asked.

"I cried a little, then I dried my eyes and declared, 'I'll go back and get it some time, for it is a pretty box and my grandfather brought it from China.' "

"And you never came back?" asked Chad.

"No, I never came back till this very week. And now I'd like someone to climb the tree and hunt for it. There was something in the box that I have reason to think is worth a good deal of money. And there was a picture of my brother in it—the only picture we had of him."

"I'll try to find it," Chad promised. "But I don't believe it's there after all these years. My sister and I have climbed all over that tree and we never saw a box of any kind. Maybe someone found it long ago and took it away."

"Might be," admitted Grandmother Hale, "but I have a hunch that it's still there, if only someone will look in all the nooks and hollows in the big tree."

"I'll hunt for it. And I'll get my sister Elaine to help me. She's good at finding things; and she likes to climb that old oak."

"A girl by the name of Elaine climb trees!" exclaimed Grandmother Hale. "She should live in a castle with turrets and towers. She should be dressed in long dresses of satins and silks. She should sit in a beautiful bower and be waited on."

"Not my sister," said Chad. "She can climb trees as well as I can. Almost as well," he added, not wanting to admit that she could do it quite as well. "But it is so long since you put the box there, are you sure that is the right tree?"

Grandmother Hale went to the front of the porch and gazed across the road at the old oak standing some distance back in the meadow.

"Yes, I'm sure that is the same tree. There were other trees near it then, but they were not oaks. And this tree looks as if it might have been here sixty years ago."

Chad was quiet for a few moments. Then he said, "You know, I don't believe we'll find a box that was left in a tree sixty years ago. All sorts of things might have happened to it. Someone might have found it very soon after you left. It might have been pushed out of the hollow by a squirrel and been picked up by someone."

"I know it," Grandmother Hale agreed.

"Then there is another thing that might have happened to it but—"

He didn't finish the sentence, for a girl came running across the road.

"This is my sister Elaine," said Chad, as she came up the steps. "We call her Ellie for short."

3. The Silver Box

GRANDMOTHER HALE looked Ellie over. "She's a likely-looking girl," she said to herself. Aloud she said, "So this is Elaine! I'm glad to see you!"

"Thank you," Ellie responded, pleased to be welcomed so heartily.

Grandmother Hale asked about their school, about their books and many other things. When Chad and Ellie had told her, she said, "Things certainly have changed since I lived here when I was about Ellie's age."

"I s'pose they have," said Chad. "Was our house built then?"

"Oh, no. This house was the only one on this road anywhere near. There were woods where your house is —great trees of the primeval forest."

"Oh-h!" Ellie exclaimed. "That would seem queer."

Grandmother Hale went on, "That big oak tree was often called 'The pirate oak.' It was near a creek that flowed down to the sea. There was a story that pirates once came up the creek and buried a chest of treasure under that tree."

"There isn't a creek there now," Chad told her. "Are you sure there used to be one?"

"Just as sure as that I sit here. We used to skate on it in the winter and sail boats on it in the spring, when the water was deep. The pirate oak stood near its head."

"I wonder what became of it," said Chad.

"It's just meadow land all around there now," Ellie explained.

"Things do change if you have been away from a place sixty years," sighed Grandmother Hale. "That creek must have been drained off."

"I guess it was," said Chad. "I wish it was there now, then we'd have a good place for skating."

Grandmother Hale was looking off up the road. "Tell me who lives in that fine big house on the other side of the road." She pointed to the Peterson house.

"Oh, that house!" Chad exclaimed. "It is empty. No one has lived in it for two or three years."

"Too bad. It looks like a nice house and not very old. Now if this house didn't have a leaky roof, I'd be very comfortable here. I like it as it is in fair weather, for it is a pleasant old-fashioned house. But when it rains hard, it leaks in the rooms upstairs, I am told."

"Oh, dear! That is too bad," Ellie exclaimed. "Couldn't you have it fixed?"

"I could, but it takes a lot of money. If only I had the silver box, that might solve the problem."

"What silver box?" Ellie inquired, just as Chad had done.

So Grandmother Hale had to tell the story again— how she left it in the old oak tree when they went west.

"And now if you two can find that silver box and if the thing is still inside that I think is there, I'll give you a handsome present and have enough left to have the house painted, put a new roof on it and do some other things that will make this a fine place to live."

"Could you tell us what is in it?" Chad asked.

"No, that isn't best. After all, I may be mistaken. I was only nine years old when we left here and may have forgotten just what that thing looked like. So no one will ever know unless the box is found. But I'll tell you what the box looks like."

She went to her dresser and brought back a pasteboard box, about five inches long and three inches wide and an inch high.

"As nearly as I can remember, it was about the size of this box," she told them. "You can see the shape. But this one is made of pasteboard, while that was made of silver, with a pretty design carved on the cover. My initials were on it too—M for Mary, W for Whitman, which was my name then."

"We'll go right over to the old oak and search for it," said Chad.

"There isn't a chance in a hundred that we'll find it, but we'll do our best," Ellie added.

They scampered across the road, climbed the low fence into the meadow and raced over to the old oak tree. Soon Chad had shinnied up the trunk and was inspecting a little hollow place in the side of it. Elaine followed close behind.

"You search in that side of the tree and I'll take this one," she said.

It was a still day. Of the thousands of leaves on the

old oak, not a leaf moved. Chad climbed from limb to limb, looking into hollow places, poking his hands into squirrels' nests, thrusting his fingers into crotches.

Once he exclaimed, "Here's something!" when he pushed his hand into a squirrel's nest. But it proved to be merely a piece of tin foil that had been blown into the hollow, perhaps from the wrapping of a candy bar in the tree house.

In the top of the tree a bird was pecking away at a big limb, stopping once in a while to scold—or so it seemed.

"I do believe that bird doesn't like to have us here," said Elaine. "It's scolding us."

Chad pulled away the leaves till he could see the bird above his head.

"It's a woodpecker," he told Ellie. "He's a pretty bird. We'd probably find a hole he has pecked in that big limb if we should climb high enough."

Ellie had brought a book with her. She sat on the floor of the tree house and leaned against a limb. She was so interested in the story that she forgot all about searching for the silver box.

Chad climbed farther up and kept looking to see if there was a little opening anywhere that might lead into a hollow.

They had been there an hour when he said to Ellie, "What's the use of our hunting any longer for that box?

Of course it isn't here after all that time since Grandmother Hale was a little girl."

"But I'd like to find it for her sake," Ellie declared. "She's nice and friendly."

"She surely is nice and friendly," Chad agreed. "But that won't bring back the silver box. Let's go home."

They slid down from their high perches and were about to start across the meadow when Chad exclaimed, "Look, Ellie! There's a moving van going into the yard of the Peterson house."

"Oh, a family moving in there!" Ellie exclaimed, all excited at the prospect of having neighbors across the field in the house that had been closed so long.

"They must be rich or they wouldn't be moving into that house," said Chad.

They stood and watched as the moving men carried furniture into the house. And when the van drove away, they raced back to Grandmother Hale's.

"Well, did you find my silver box?" she asked, as Ellie came in the door, out of breath from running so fast.

"No, not a glimpse of it."

"There are several hollow places in the old tree, but no silver box in any of them," Chad added.

Then Ellie came out with the big news. "There's a family moving into that big house on the other side of the road—the Peterson place!"

"That's fine," said Grandmother Hale. "It will be nice to see lights in the windows."

4. New Neighbors

THE NEXT day Chad spent most of his time with his stamp collection. Ellie helped Mother put the dish cupboard in order, then read *Heidi* for the third time.

In the afternoon Mother had to go into town for a teachers' meeting. When she came home it was raining hard. After she got off the bus she had to walk through the storm for a quarter of a mile, so, in spite of her umbrella, she was drenched by the time she reached home.

"Oh, dear! Oh, dear!" said Ellie. She ran to get dry shoes and stockings for Mother. Chad took the umbrella and put it to drip.

"I wish we had a car, then you wouldn't have to get drenched like this," said Chad.

"It would be fine if we could have one," said Mother. "If wishes were horses, beggars might ride."

The following morning was bright and sunny. "I'll beat you to the old oak, Ellie!" cried Chad, when he had finished pulling weeds in the aster bed.

Suiting the action to the word, he pushed through the break in the hedge and scooted across the meadow. Ellie couldn't quite keep up with him, but she wasn't far behind.

As Chad scrambled up the trunk of the tree, a squirrel on a high limb chattered and scolded and a blue jay screeched.

Ellie followed and quickly pulled herself up to the tree house. When she had taken her seat on the floor of it, she saw a woodpecker higher up. His red-crested head bobbed back and forth and his stiff tail jerked up and down as he struck into the hard wood with his bill.

"There are a lot of interesting things going on in a big tree," she said, after watching the woodpecker for a few minutes.

"Sure are," Chad agreed. "But let's hunt for the silver box some more. Maybe if we thump along the bark of the trunk and the big limbs, we'll find some place that might be hiding it. Sometimes the bark grows over a hollow place and covers it."

Ellie was looking out through the branches at the house beyond the meadow. "I guess our new neighbors are rich," she said. "Just see the nice lace curtains at the windows."

"And look at the big car in the driveway!" Chad exclaimed.

"There's a boy about our age," said Ellie, a little later. "See! He's standing on the side porch of the big house, looking this way!"

Evidently he could hear their voices, for he certainly couldn't see them, hidden as they were by the foliage.

"Come on over!" Chad shouted, in a friendly tone.

The boy needed no second invitation. He came slowly, though, walking across the grass instead of running, as Chad would have done. A short distance away he stopped.

"How did you get up there?" he asked.

"We climbed. Come on up," Ellie invited him cordially.

The boy walked close to the trunk of the tree to see who had called. His smart clothes and his polished shoes were in great contrast to Chad's old sport suit and play shoes.

"How do you climb a tree as big as this," the boy asked. "There's nothing to take hold of."

"Oh yes, there are lots of things. There are little humps to step on and some twigs to grasp, to pull yourself up by," Ellie explained.

The boy started to climb, but soon slipped back.

"I'll come down and help you," Chad called to him. "There is a little knack to it. If you are not used to climbing trees, it isn't easy."

"You never can climb a tree safely in those smooth shoes," Ellie told him. "Can't you put some rubber-soled shoes on?"

"Why, yes, I have some," the boy replied.

"You'd better run home and put them on," Chad told him.

The boy ran home and changed his shoes. When he came back, a few minutes later, Chad slid down to help him.

"I'll boost and you pull yourself up by that little branch," he explained.

In a few minutes, with Chad helping, the boy had reached the tree house and was sitting on the floor of it, holding to a limb for dear life.

"You'll get used to it after a while," Ellie said, from her perch on a nearby limb.

"What is your name?" Chad asked.

"Wilfred. Wilfred Mansfield."

"Nice name," Ellie commented. "What are you called for short?"

"For short? I'm always called Wilfred. And the chauffeur calls me Master Wilfred."

"Oh-h!" was Chad's only comment.

"As I said, you'll get used to climbing after you have done it a few times," Ellie went on. "Watch."

With that she stood up on the limb on which she had been sitting, reached for the one above and swung herself up. "See! It's easy," she said.

"Aw, that's nothing," said Wilfred. "I could do it, only I don't want to try right now."

A little later he remarked, "I'll bet we have something you folks haven't got."

"What is it?" Chad asked.

"A television set."

"That's fine," said Ellie, with hopes of being asked over to see a broadcast. "I wish we had one. We do have a radio."

"So do we. Our set cost six hundred dollars," Wilfred bragged. "We can get any station, all over the world."

"And I see you folks have a fine big car," said Chad.

"Oh, yes. It cost five thousand dollars. There's a big radio in that, too."

"It's a splendid car," Ellie agreed. "I'm glad you can have such a nice one."

"We have two other cars," he boasted. "How many cars has your family got?"

Ellie hesitated before replying. "We haven't any car. Maybe we'll get one next year."

"How will you get a car next year if you haven't any money to get one this year?" Wilfred insisted.

"We might have some good luck," Chad answered.

Ellie said without thinking, "We might find the silver box."

"What silver box? Where is it?" demanded Wilfred.

"That's what we'd like to know," Ellie replied. "It might be somewhere in this very tree."

"Do you mean it?" demanded Wilfred, excited at such news.

"Don't tell anyone," Ellie begged him, alarmed that she had let the cat out of the bag. "It's a secret."

"It probably isn't here any more," Chad told him, wanting to make him forget about it. In a moment he called out, "Here's a queer bug, up here on a twig. I never saw one like it before."

"There are lots of interesting things in a tree," Ellie said, hoping that Wilfred would get interested in some of them and forget what she had said. So she chattered on about how wonderful it was that the old oak had lived and kept on growing for two hundred years.

"It's wonderful how a tree can make these beautiful leaves," she said. "These pretty acorns, too."

But Wilfred was not to be put off. "This tree doesn't belong to you," he said in a loud voice. He put his hand up to brush away an insect that had flown against his forehead.

"Why no, it doesn't belong to us," Ellie admitted. "But we've always played here and climbed it all we wanted to."

Chad had chimed in, "We know that it isn't ours. I don't know who owns this field now. Our family used to own it, but after our father died, our mother sold it to someone who lives away from here. But surely anyone can climb a tree if he doesn't break off the little limbs or do any harm to it."

"We are very careful," Ellie put in. "We don't break off the twigs. We don't peel off the bark. You can't harm a strong old tree like this one, not by just climbing around in it."

"It's ours now," Wilfred told them. "My father was the one who bought this field. And we don't want anyone climbing our trees or trespassing on our land."

Ellie nearly fell off the limb in astonishment.

"Do you mean we can't climb this tree any more?" she demanded with flashing eyes.

"That's just what I mean," Wilfred said in a determined tone of voice.

Chad and Ellie couldn't believe their ears.

"You'd better get down now," said Wilfred.

There was a moment of complete silence, then Chad said in a low tone, "We'd better go, Ellie. Maybe he'll change his mind by tomorrow."

They quietly climbed down and walked away. As they went with reluctant feet across the meadow toward their own home, Ellie said, "What is the matter with that boy?"

"Meanie!" Chad said in as rough a tone as he could manage.

5. The Flashlight

ELLIE slept late the next morning. When she wakened, she found that Chad had gone to the town to do an errand for Mother.

She could not think at first what it was that made her feel sad. Then, as she went downstairs, she remembered what had happened the day before. The old oak! They couldn't have fun there any more.

After breakfast, she asked Mother if there was anything she could do to help about the place.

"Yes, there is something. Some of the flowers need picking. You may pick all the blossoms that are full blown. Throw away those that have begun to fade. Bring the good ones in and arrange them in vases, to make the rooms pretty."

Ellie loved to pick flowers and make bouquets. She took the garden shears and a basket and went first to the bed of asters. There were white ones and purple ones and pink ones. Such large beautiful flowers they were!

Ellie was sorry she hadn't picked them sooner, there were so many that had faded and had to be thrown away. Frosty followed her around the flower beds, sniffing at a blossom now and then.

Once in a while Ellie looked over toward the oak tree. In a few minutes she saw someone going toward it. On a second look she saw who it was.

"Why, there's Wilfred going to the old oak! I wonder if he's going to try to climb it all alone," she said to herself. "If he does, I hope he'll fall out."

But soon she was sorry she had thought it even for a moment. Ellie could not long hold a grudge.

She watched as Wilfred stood a short distance away

looking up at the great tree. Chad came home and ran out to the garden.

"What are you looking at?" he asked, seeing her gazing so intently across the meadow.

"Oh, Chad, Wilfred is going to try to climb the tree alone. I'm afraid he'll fall."

They both watched as he went over to the big rough trunk of the tree and tried to climb it. They watched as he managed to get up a few feet and almost reached the lowest limb. But not quite. He slid back to the ground.

"Oh, dear! He can't make it," she cried.

"I'd go over and help him if he weren't so mean," Chad said.

They saw the boy standing a few minutes looking at the huge tree, evidently pondering what to do. Then he went toward his own home.

"He's given up," said Ellie. "I wouldn't give two cents for a boy who gives up easily."

But he had not given up. Before long he came back, tugging something larger than himself, at least longer than he was tall.

"A ladder!" exclaimed Chad.

Wilfred placed it against the big trunk. They could see him go slowly up to the top of the ladder, then crawl over to the tree house.

There he sat for a long time, "all by his lonesome,"

as Ellie said. "I should think he'd have a better time if he had some friends to enjoy it with him," she added.

"So would I," said Chad heartily.

"He doesn't dare go any farther up," Ellie said, after several minutes had passed and the boy still sat there. "Fraidy cat!"

Chad went through the hedge and part way over to the oak tree and called to Wilfred, "I'll come over and show you how to climb high if you want me to."

"Oh, no. You just keep away from this tree," came the answer.

"Selfish!" cried Ellie, when Chad came back. "He doesn't deserve to have that grand tree all to himself."

"Let's go over to see Grandmother Hale and tell her how things stand," Chad proposed.

They found her in the dining room arranging dishes in the cupboard. When they had told her all about it, she said, "There are all sorts of folks in the world. Some are selfish, some are unselfish. You take my word for it that Wilfred will find out some time that it doesn't pay to be selfish."

The next morning Ellie was wakened before daylight by a rooster crowing loudly under her window. He crowed twice and flapped his wings.

"There! That's enough," she cried, as she turned over and tried to go to sleep.

In a moment there was a third loud crow. Ellie got up and went to the window. "Shoo! Scat! Go off!" she scolded.

Slowly and proudly old Peter walked away. But Ellie, looking across the meadow, saw something that made her exclaim, "A light! And I do believe it is near the pirate oak."

She stood at the window a few minutes. The light would flash on a few seconds, go off, flash on, go off.

"It must be a flashlight," she decided.

She hurried down the hall and called Chad. "Wake up, Chad! There's something queer in the old oak."

"Oh-h!" he murmured, then turned over and went to sleep again.

Ellie didn't want to waken Mother by calling loud, so she pulled a lock of Chad's hair.

"Ouch! Go off!" he cried.

But Ellie persisted. "Wake up, Chad! Come and see something strange," she whispered in his ear. "There's a light near the old oak."

With that he sat up and demanded, "Who's in the old oak?"

"I don't know. There's a light there—a flashlight."

She ran back to the window and Chad followed quickly. They stood in the darkness and tried to look across the meadow. Nothing could be seen clearly, but it was so near morning that there was a faint glow in the east.

Soon they saw a flash of light, then another—and another, near the trunk of the tree, several feet from the ground.

"Gee whillikens!" Chad cried in a low voice. "I believe someone is standing at the foot of the tree, reaching up as high as he can to see if there is a hollow place in the trunk, with something hidden in it. But why does he come so early in the morning?"

"It couldn't be Wilfred," said Ellie. "He'd be too scared to go there at night."

"No; it can't be Wilfred. It's someone taller."

"Do you s'pose he's heard about the silver box? Why else would anyone want to go there in the dark?"

Mother appeared at the door. "Why are you children up at this time of night?" she demanded.

"There's something queer," Ellie replied.

"Come here, Mom, and look over toward the old oak," Chad said.

She came and stood with them at the window. "Why, of all things! A flashlight near that tree at night! Why would anyone come then? Who in the world could it be?"

"My guess is that it's someone who has heard about the silver box and is sneaking there at night to hunt for it," Chad replied.

"But there isn't one chance in a thousand that it is there after all these years."

"I know it," Chad agreed. "I know it, but if it should be there, Grandmother Hale should have it and not someone else."

Dawn was creeping over the earth. The sky became rosy. Streaks of pink light began to stream up toward the zenith.

"A sunrise is pretty," said Ellie softly.

"Look!" Chad exclaimed in great excitement.

There was a man coming away from the tree. He put something in a leather bag that hung from his shoulder. He stood a few moments under the tree, looking up at the trunk, then walked slowly over toward the road.

"I'm going over to ask him what he was there for," Chad said, starting back to his own room to dress.

"You'd better not," Mother said gently. "We know nothing of what sort of man he is. If he has found something valuable, he'll not easily give it up, after taking all that trouble to get it."

Chad went back to his room, and from his window saw the man get into a car and drive away toward the village. He couldn't go to sleep for wondering what the man was up to, so after a bit he dressed and went down to the front porch.

After breakfast, Chad and Ellie ran over to Grand-mother Hale's and told her about it.

"Hum-m!" she said, "queer that the man came in the night. Maybe that is the end of my silver box."

6. *Hunting for Treasure*

THE NEXT evening Chad set the alarm-clock for four o'clock.

"I'll get up awful early so I can be sure to see that man if he comes again," he thought as he wound the alarm. "If he does come, I'll go over and ask him what he's doing in that tree at night. I'll ask him, 'How come?'"

Chad felt very brave, winding the clock in the safety of his own bedroom. Having finished, he looked carefully to see if he had set it at exactly the right time. Yes, there was the little hand of the alarm at exactly four on the small dial.

He put the clock under his pillow so no one else would hear it. Then he went to bed and into the land of dreams. When he heard the alarm ring the next morning, he thought it was the sound of sleigh bells, for he was dreaming that it was winter and he was riding in a sleigh, as he had last winter when he visited Uncle John.

Then he remembered. It was four o'clock and he must get up. He shut off the alarm, switched on the light and went across the hall to a window in the store-room.

Darkness covered the earth. Not a thing could he see except a few stars in the sky.

He kept very quiet and listened. Not a sound could he hear except the twitter of small birds in the trees and shrubbery.

He glanced in the direction of the pirate oak. "Nothing doing," he decided, as he could see nothing in the dense darkness.

But in a moment there was a flash of light, then another.

"Jiminy cricket! There is somebody under the tree this morning!" he exclaimed, half aloud.

In a short time he had made up his mind. "I'm going just through the hedge. Maybe I can see from there what he is doing. He can't be up to any good, sneaking around in the dark."

Chad didn't want to waken anyone, not even Ellie, this time, so he tiptoed over to his room as quietly as possible, dressed as fast as he could, put out the light and crept slowly and carefully downstairs.

Some of the stairs creaked so loudly that he was worried lest Mother should hear him. When part way down, he imagined he heard a door opened in the upper hall. He stopped a few seconds and stood as still as a statue.

Because he tried to be so quiet, it took him much longer than usual. By the time he had pushed through the break in the hedge, a bit of morning light was showing in the eastern sky.

He stood still a few moments, looking toward the tree, which was still in darkness. Then came a flash of light.

"Jeepers!" Chad said under his breath.

He started across the meadow, but all at once he stopped. The morning light enabled him to see clearer.

The man was not up in the tree, but was digging in the ground under it!

"Jeepers!" exclaimed Chad again. "What is he digging for?"

Astonished at this turn of things, he stood a few moments rooted to the spot. He saw the man turn up a spadeful of earth, then another and another. For several minutes he kept digging in one spot.

Evidently he did not find what he was digging for, so he went to another place. Chad watched as he kept throwing up dirt till he had spaded half way around the tree, but several feet away from it.

Chad went slowly across the meadow to within a few rods of the old oak and stood near a clump of bushes, where he could quickly hide if he wanted to.

The rising sun was making the eastern sky all rosy, but it was still dim where Chad stood in the shadow. Soon he saw the man gather up the spade and flashlight, and start away.

Instead of going over to the road, the man went the other way, toward the back of the meadow, and climbed over the fence into a wheatfield covered with stubble.

"I'll follow him," Chad decided. "I'll find out whether he found anything buried in the ground."

He ran to the fence, climbed over it and started on

through the prickly stubble. The man had long legs and was a fast walker, so Chad kept falling behind.

He started to run, but a stone hidden in the weeds made him stumble and go headlong into a thistle patch. Picking himself up, he rubbed the dirt from his knees and again started to run.

Then Chad saw that the man had climbed over the next fence and was in the clearing at the edge of the woods.

"Shucks! I'll never catch up with him," Chad began to think. But he still hurried on, over the rough ground.

In the clearing, a twisting path ran here and there, around underbrush, across a little brook. Chad tried to keep the man in sight. Once he called out, "Hey, Mister!" But he was not near enough to make himself heard. So he hurried and called again.

The man turned. "What are you following me for?" he asked gruffly.

"Why were you digging under the old oak?" Chad asked. "Did you find anything?"

The man looked sternly at Chad as he replied, "I have as much right to the pirate's treasure as anyone else." His face was dark and ugly.

"Oh, maybe," Chad admitted.

"If I did find it, I wouldn't tell you," the man de-

clared. "And you'd better get away from here quick. It's nobody's business whether I found the treasure."

Chad didn't like that tone. He didn't like the looks of that face. He turned and ran as fast as his legs could carry him. And he never stopped until he had climbed over the fence into the wheatfield.

Chad puzzled his head all the way back to the old oak. Then he stood and looked at the ground under the tree. "Jeepers!" he said aloud. "He's spoiled all that nice grass!"

He didn't hurry home, for no one would be up, or so he thought. He went out to the road instead of through the gap in the hedge. And when he looked over toward Grandmother Hale's house, there she was, sitting on the porch, reading a book!

Chad crossed the road and went up to the porch. She was so intent on what she was reading that she didn't see him till he said, "Good morning!"

"Why, good morning! Why are you up so early?" she asked.

"I saw a man digging under the old oak and I followed him."

"Sakes alive!" exclaimed Grandmother Hale. "Haven't folks forgotten that old story about there being buried treasure there?"

She put her book down and said, "Come up here on

the porch, Chad, and I'll tell you more about it."

Chad took his seat on the front edge of the porch and leaned against a post, looking up at Grandmother Hale.

"As I told you, when I was a little girl that tree was called the pirate oak," she began. "Sometimes in those days men would come there and dig in the ground hoping to find that treasure. But I supposed everyone had forgotten all about it."

"Do you think the old story was true?" Chad asked eagerly.

"It might be. There used to be pirates on the ocean. Sometimes they came ashore on Long Island and buried their treasure. I suppose they might have buried some under this oak tree. It would have been a handy place."

"Do you think there might be treasure there now?" Chad's eyes sparkled, as they always did when he was excited.

"I don't know. Anyway, I hope men won't keep digging in the ground under that nice tree. They spoil the grass and they might cut the roots. I hope that man won't come again."

"I hope not," Chad agreed.

"Have you had any breakfast?" she asked.

"Nope; I was in such a hurry that I didn't stop to eat."

"Go to the kitchen, Chad, and get a glass of milk

from the ice box. And there are some doughnuts in the cake box. Help yourself."

"Thank you. I am hungry, now I come to think of it."

When he came back, with the glass of milk in one hand and three doughnuts in the other, they talked about many things. Chad stayed till he heard the clock strike seven. "I'll have to go home now," he said.

"Come again," Grandmother Hale invited him, as he ran down the steps.

Breakfast was an exciting time that morning, with Chad telling about his adventure following the man who had been digging for treasure. He ended by saying, "I'm going to take a spade and dig there. Want to help me, Ellie? Maybe we could find the treasure."

"Sure," she replied.

They each took along a spade and a rake. And they dug a hole deeper than any the man had dug. Then Chad's spade hit something hard. For a few moments he was all excited.

"Aw, it's only a root of the tree," he said on looking closer.

They tried again, in another spot. Again Chad hit something hard; but it proved to be a stone.

"Let's quit," said Ellie, wiping the perspiration from

her face. "I'd much rather climb the tree than dig in the ground."

Before leaving they put the earth back in the holes that had been dug, then raked the rough ground and patted it smooth with their spades.

7. The Morning Trip

THAT DAY it rained, beginning in the early afternoon, though it stopped before evening. Chad thought no one would go to the tree in the wet grass, so he didn't set the alarm.

In the morning, before daylight, Ellie was wakened

again by the old rooster crowing under her window. She wanted to have a chance to sleep some more, so she went to the window and cried, "Stop it! Go off!"

When old Peter paid no attention, she went across the hall to the guest room to find something to throw at the noisy creature. The guest room was on the side of the house toward the meadow. As Ellie passed the window her eyes caught sight of a light in the pirate oak.

"There's that flashlight again," she murmured.

She stood at the window a few moments, eagerly looking across at the oak.

"There it is again," she exclaimed. "I must call Chad."

She hurried down the hall. "Chad! Wake up! The light is in the old oak again!"

She whispered softly, so as not to waken Mother, who was sleeping in the next room.

"What's that? The flashlight in the tree again?"

"Yes; I can see it from the window in the guest room."

In a jiffy Chad was in there.

"Sure enough! But he's not digging. He's reaching up the trunk of the tree. I wonder why."

The light would flash on, go off, flash on, go off.

Chad ran to his room, slipped on his play suit and was down the stairs in a hurry.

Ellie went back to her room. The rooster was still crowing every minute or two, but she paid no attention. She dressed quickly, went downstairs quietly and joined Chad at the hedge.

Except for the flashing of the light, they would not have known just where the oak tree stood.

"Could it be a firefly?" Ellie asked, as the strange light appeared and disappeared.

"No; fireflies have gone back to bed before this time of night. They come out in the evening. They dance around mostly in bushes near the ground."

They spoke softly, so anyone near the oak would not hear their voices.

Dawn began to show in the east. Birds chirped in the trees around them. An airplane roared above their heads.

"It's pleasant in the morning," Ellie remarked.

"Lazy folks never see the sun rise," said Chad.

Great streamers of rosy light were soon stretching up from the horizon in the east. The white clouds were turning pink. A golden light was glowing around the spot where the sun would come up.

Soon it was light enough to see the old oak. It stood beautiful and stately there in the meadow.

"Look! There's the flashlight again!" Ellie exclaimed.

"And there's a man coming away from the tree!" cried Chad, in great excitement.

They watched with all their eyes. They saw him open a leather bag that hung from his shoulder and put something in it, something that glittered in the morning light.

"The silver box!" Ellie exclaimed.

"I wonder," said Chad.

They saw the man start across the meadow toward the road in front of their house. Chad ran forward a short distance.

"That's the man who was here the first time, the one who went away in a car!" he exclaimed. But this time he had no car. He went on foot down the road toward the village.

"I'm going to follow him," said Chad. "Tell Mother I'll be back as soon as I can."

"Can't I go too?" Ellie asked eagerly.

"Better not. There's no knowing how far I'll have to go."

And he ran down the road toward the village.

The man was a fast walker and had a head start. Chad ran at first, hoping to overtake him. Soon he became tired, stopped running and walked swiftly in the middle of the road. There were not many cars at that time of morning.

When the man came to the edge of the village, Chad saw him turn in at one of the houses.

"That's Professor Pratt's house!" Chad exclaimed. "And it is the Professor himself!"

Professor Pratt was a teacher in the high school where Mother taught. He was surprised when Chad came up with him.

"Well, well, Chad, why are you up so early in the morning? And why are you following me all the way home?"

"Oh, sir, I wondered what you were doing at the old oak so early in the morning, before daybreak."

Professor Pratt smiled. "Maybe I like to get up early in the morning and take a walk in the country."

"Oh! Was that all?" Chad demanded.

"No, not quite. In fact I was looking for something."

"Were you looking for the silver box? And did you find it?"

"The silver box? What silver box?"

"One that was put in the tree a long time ago. It was shaped like this." Chad showed with his thumbs and fingers.

"How did you know I was there?" the Professor asked.

"We saw the flashlight, my sister and I."

"I see. And up so early in the morning! Well, I

didn't find a silver box. I didn't find *any* box, but I have a tin box in this leather bag, a box that I took there."

"Oh-h!" said Chad, greatly mystified. Then he added, "But you must have been hunting for something."

"Yes, I was hunting for something. And I found it."

He opened the bag and took out a little square box about six inches across. It shone like polished silver.

"Gee whillikens!" Chad exclaimed. "That looks a bit like the one I have been hunting for in the old oak."

"This is only tin," said the Professor. "But there is something very interesting inside. Want to look in?"

"Sure," was the quick reply.

"Come with me. I'll let you take a peek."

8. *The Creature in a Box*

CHAD followed him up the steps onto a side porch and into the house. They entered a room that contained a large desk, some filing cases and many books on shelves along the walls.

The Professor took the cover from the box and said,

"Look in there. Tell me what you see."

"Why, it's a butterfly!" Chad exclaimed. "It has beautiful wings."

"It does look like a butterfly, but it is something else," the man explained. "It is a moth. They look much alike, for they both have wings."

"Gee!" Chad exclaimed. "It surely is pretty."

"Yes, that is one of the most beautiful moths I ever saw. I have been wanting a specimen of it for a long time."

Chad looked surprised. "Why would you want a moth?" he asked. "My mother tries to get rid of them."

"But this isn't the kind that your mother tries to get rid of. Those are small and eat woolen clothes. This one flies around outdoors in the night."

"Oh," said Chad. "But why do you want it?"

"I'm making a collection of moths. Maybe you make a collection of something. Eh?"

"Why, yes; I have a stamp collection. I like to get rare stamps."

"Lots of boys do. Well, I collect moths. I'm a Naturalist. I study moths and other creatures."

"It must be fun," said Chad.

"Yes, of course. Last evening I went sugaring for moths on that old oak tree. Maybe you saw me there, just after sunset."

"Sugaring for moths? What does that mean?" Chad wanted to know. "I didn't see you there last evening, but we did see you this morning. We saw your flashlight."

"Have you never been told about sugaring for moths?"

"No."

"Moths like sweet things to eat. We can catch them by putting something sweet on the trunk of a tree. Sometimes we brush molasses there, sometimes a sugary syrup mixed with something that has a smell that will attract them, like strong cider. You'd be surprised to see how many will come when I put something sweet on a tree trunk."

"Then you catch them?"

"You have guessed it, Sonny. But we can't catch them just any time. We must put the sweet stuff there about dark and leave it all night. Last evening I went there just before dark. I stood on the ground and reached up as far as I could and put some syrup on the trunk of the old oak. This morning I went just before daylight," the Professor went on. "I had to have a flashlight then."

"Yes, that's when we saw it," said Chad.

"I saw your tree house up in that old tree. Nice places, tree houses. I remember the one the Robinson boys had in *The Swiss Family Robinson.*"

"Oh, did you read that story?" asked Chad, interested at once.

"Sure. Did you?"

"Yes, three times."

For a few minutes they talked about the interesting things in that book. It made them feel like friends.

"When we saw your light this morning, we thought someone was hunting for the silver box," Chad told him. "That is why I went part way over there."

Then of course he had to tell a little about Grandmother Hale's silver box.

"It might possibly be in the tree still," said the Professor. "But my guess is that if it is still there, the bark has grown around it, so you'll never find it, not unless lightning should strike the tree and tear off the bark."

Chad looked once more at the beautiful creature in the box. "I'd like to see one of those creatures fly," he said.

"You'd have to go outdoors in the night," said the Professor. "They are more beautiful when they fly. This kind has two pairs of wings. Those you see are the upper ones. They are not very colorful, just a soft gray. But when the moth spreads its wings to fly, the under wings show. They are some pretty color—red or blue or yellow. This one's under wings are red. In fact, it is called a Catocala, which means 'under wings.' Sometime I'll take you with me if you want to go along when I am hunting moths."

"I sure would," said Chad eagerly.

"You may find that silver box sometime if you keep looking. Sixty years is a long time, but it isn't impossible that the box is still there."

Chad turned his attention again to the moth. "What are you going to do with it?" he asked.

"I'll show it to my students, then I'll mount it for my collection. And I'll write about it. I write books about insects—moths and butterflies mostly."

They talked a few minutes longer, then Professor Pratt said, "I'm glad to have seen you this morning, Chad. And now I must eat breakfast and go to work."

"I'm sorry I suspected you of stealing the silver box," said Chad. "But you see that it is quite important that we don't let it be carried off by someone. Ellie and I want to get it for Grandmother Hale if we can."

"Quite right, sonny, quite right. Good luck to you. If you will come back in a few days, I'll show you some more of these pretty creatures."

They said good-bye and Chad gave one more look at the moth before he left. He went home by a shorter way, but even so, it was so late that Mother and Ellie were eating their breakfast.

"For goodness sake, where have you been all this time?" Mother asked.

Chad told her about his adventure. "Professor Pratt is a very interesting man," he said. "He told me a lot about moths. He wants me to put molasses on the trunk of the old oak sometime and see if I can get a specimen of rare moths for him."

"I wish I could have gone with you," Elaine sighed. "You have all the fun."

9. *No Trespassing*

AFTER breakfast, Chad found Grandmother Hale in her side yard, tying up the morning-glory vines.

"My lovely morning-glories were knocked down by the wind last night," she told him. "I came out just now to tie them up to the side of the house. Do you want to help me?"

"Sure I'll help," was Chad's quick reply. "How shall I do it?"

"You can stand on this high stool and tie the vines to those nails you will find on the side of the house. Morning-glories don't like to lie on the earth. They like to climb."

Chad placed the stool close to the house and climbed up on it. Grandmother Hale handed him one of the strings with the morning-glory vine twisted around it.

"Fasten that tight to the nail at the left end," she said.

Having tied the string to the nail, Chad took the end of the vine and carefully curled it around the string.

"The vine will cling by itself, once it is started right," Grandmother Hale told him.

"Gee! They are pretty things!" Chad exclaimed, as he looked closely at the large blue blossom he was gently fastening in its right place.

"Heavenly Blue these are called," Grandmother Hale told him. "No prettier flower grows."

Chad was so interested in getting the flowers properly fixed that he didn't begin at once to tell her about his adventure of the morning. Then, all at once he recalled it.

"Did you see anything queer near the old oak this morning?" he suddenly asked.

"No; what would there be in the old oak this morning that isn't there every morning?"

"A light. A flashlight. Ellie and I saw it from a window, before sunrise."

"That is strange," she said. "Who could have been there?"

She took her seat in a garden chair and said, "Now tell me all about it, Chad."

He told her about seeing the flashlight near the tree. He told her about the beautiful sunrise that slowly lighted up the earth. He told about the man who stood reaching up high on the trunk of the tree and the tin box that glittered in the morning light.

"Gracious me!" she exclaimed. "It might have been my box!"

"But it wasn't. I followed the man toward the village. It turned out to be Professor Pratt. I went with him right into his house and found out what was in the box. What do you think?"

"I never could guess. Tell me."

"A moth. A beautiful big moth."

"Why on earth would he want a moth? I detest them. They eat clothes."

"Not that kind," Chad told her. "They just fly around in the night and look pretty."

"But why would he put it in a tin box?"

"For his collection," Chad replied.

He sat on an upturned box and told her all about his adventure of the morning, from the time of first seeing the flashlight to the moment when he saw the pretty creature in the tin box.

"You didn't tell him about my silver box, did you?"

"I had to tell him a little, but if he should find it, he wouldn't keep it. He's all right. He'd give it to you."

When he finished, Grandmother Hale had to attend to some beans she was cooking and Chad started mowing the front lawn for her. When it was all done, she gave him three sugar cookies and a glass of milk. "Thank you too," she said.

As he was sitting on the porch eating the cookies, she reached into her pocket and took out a piece of paper on which something was written.

"Since we have been talking about trees so much, I thought you might like to hear a poem about them," she said. "I found it in an old book and copied it. It's by a man named Henry Fothergill Chorley. If you'd care to hear it, I'll read it to you."

"Sure I'd like to hear it," Chad replied.

In his heart he wasn't so sure, for he would rather climb a tree than hear a poem about it. But he didn't want to hurt her feelings, so he settled down to listen.

Grandmother Hale had a lovely voice and was a good reader, so Chad was soon enjoying the poem.

The Brave Old Oak

A song to the oak, the brave old oak,
   Who hath ruled in the greenwood long;
Here's health and renown to his broad green crown,
   And his fifty arms so strong.
There's fear in his frown when the sun goes down,
   And the fire in the west fades out;
And he showeth his might on a wild midnight,
   When the storms through his branches shout.

Then here's to the oak, the brave old oak,
   Who stands in his pride alone!
And still flourish he, a hale green tree,
   When a hundred years are gone!

Chad was quiet for a moment after she finished reading.

"That's a fine poem," he said finally.

"I think so," said Grandmother Hale. "If I could write a poem, I'm sure I would like to write one about trees. What would the earth be without them?"

Chad had never thought of that before. "Why, it wouldn't be very pretty," he said. "I'd miss that old oak a lot if it should die or be blown over by the wind."

They were still talking about trees when Chad suddenly rose and stood looking across the meadow. He saw Wilfred going toward the old oak with something in his arms, something rather large.

"I wonder what Wilfred is carrying," he said.

"I can't see from here? What does it look like?" Grandmother Hale asked.

"I'll go over there and find out."

Chad waited a few minutes. The boy seemed to be shoving something into the ground.

"It's a sign!" he exclaimed. "There's an upright stick standing in the ground and a crosspiece nailed to it. And there are letters on it."

"Can you see what it says?" asked Grandmother Hale.

"No; but I'll find out."

He crossed the road and walked toward the sign. It was a bit hard to read because the letters had been put on by hand and they were crooked. Chad was trying to make them out when a voice called out, "Do you see that sign?"

It was Wilfred, who by this time had climbed up into the old oak and was sitting in the tree house.

Since Chad didn't reply at once, he called again, "Do you see that sign?"

"Sure."

"What does it say?"

Chad had to study the crooked letters a few moments before he could see what they meant.

"You've spelled it wrong," he replied. "But I s'pose it means 'No Trespassing.'"

"Do you know what those words mean?"

"Yes. It means that folks must keep off, not go past it."

"It surely does mean just that," said Wilfred. "If you or your sister come nearer to this tree than that sign, you'll wish you hadn't."

"Oh-h!" Chad said, ending the word with a whistle. "Does your father know about this sign?"

"No; he's away on a long trip."

Chad started to go past the sign, just to show he would do as he pleased about it. Then he thought better of it and stepped back a few feet.

Elaine came running across the meadow. "Are we going to play in the old oak today?" she asked.

"No, I guess not. Maybe we'll never play in it again. Look at that sign."

She looked a long time at the crooked straggling letters. "Oh, dear!" she murmured. "Oh, dear!"

They both went back to Grandmother Hale's. She could tell when she saw them coming that something unpleasant was on their minds.

"What does that sign say?" she asked.

"It says, 'No trespassing,' so we can't climb the old oak any more," Elaine reported.

"Humph!" she exclaimed. "That boy is getting mighty uppity. He'd better watch out."

10. *Change of Heart*

Every little while that day Chad or Ellie looked long-
ingly toward the old oak. Once Chad decided to take a
chance. "I'm going over there, right past that sign," he
said. "Maybe I won't be discovered if I climb up quick
enough."

But he had not even reached the sign when Wilfred appeared and called out, "What are you doing, trespassing on our land?"

Chad went back to the porch, where Ellie was making a dress for her doll.

"He's a mean, contemptible boy," she said. She rolled the word under her tongue. "Contemptible, that's what he is. Insists on having that nice tree all to himself. Selfish and mean he is."

"It's a nice cool place on a hot day," said Chad. "But the worst of it is that we can't go there any more to hunt for the silver box."

To pass away the time he brought out his stamp collection. He looked through the albums and pasted a number of stamps in the right places.

Ellie never could see any fun in collecting stamps. "Just little pieces of paper," she said. "Some of them are pretty, I'll admit, but I'd rather make a new dress for my doll. I'll make her a stylish outfit."

Chad had his stamps spread out on a little table at one end of the porch. She kept working at a little table at the other end of the porch with needle and thread and scissors.

All at once Chad called to her, "Here's an interesting stamp! Want to see it? I mean that here's a picture of it. Every stamp collector wishes he could find one."

Ellie laid down her needle and thread and came over to him. Chad pointed to the picture of a stamp that had a few letters on it, the name of a town, and a picture of George Washington.

"I don't think that is so very pretty," she said.

"Who said it was? A pretty picture isn't what makes a stamp worth a lot. But that stamp is very rare. There are only one or two known in all the world."

Ellie looked at it with more interest. "I still don't see why it's worth more than lots of others."

"I'll tell you. That stamp was not only one of the very early ones. It was made and used even before the Government made the very first postage stamp. It was made by a postmaster in a certain place, not by the Government down in Washington. So it's called a postmaster stamp."

"It would be nice to have one," Ellie agreed.

"Nice? It would be wonderful. Just a few towns issued them. And most of the stamps were thrown away or got lost by the people who received them. Why didn't some of our family save one of those stamps? Gumps!"

"How could you get one?" Ellie asked. "Can't you buy one?"

Chad looked at her in amazement. "Don't you know

that it's worth a lot of money?" he said.

"Oh, dear! Then you can never have one, can you?" Ellie asked.

"Probably not. Some folks find one among old letters —in an old trunk or something."

"But we haven't any very old letters, have we?"

"Yes, we have two or three bundles of letters written a long time ago. I've looked through them many times; but there isn't one of those old stamps among them," he sighed.

Ellie went back to making her doll's dress. Chad closed his stamp albums and took them into the house. Just as he came out on the porch again there was a scream, a terrible scream, from the direction of the pirate oak.

Chad looked at Ellie. She looked at Chad.

"Gee whillikens!" he said. "Who was that?"

"Could it be Wilfred?" Ellie asked.

"Let's go and see," said Chad.

With that he ran to the hedge and pushed through it, Ellie following close at his heels.

When they came to the big sign, Ellie stopped. "Dare we go past it?" she asked.

"Come on," said Chad.

They found Wilfred lying on the ground under the oak tree, white and still.

"Jeepers!" Chad exclaimed. "I wonder if his heart is beating."

He put his ear to Wilfred's heart.

"No wonder he fell out of the tree, with those slippery shoes on," said Ellie. "Can you hear his heart beat?"

"Yes, it's beating all right," Chad reported. "But he must have been knocked unconscious." He applied all the first aid he had learned in his Boy Scout training. At last Wilfred opened his eyes. "Where am I?" he inquired in a feeble voice.

"You fell out of the tree. Where do you hurt most?"

"All over, I guess."

His eyes went shut again. Chad bent over him.

"You'd better go over and tell his mother," Chad said to Ellie.

She was about to start when Wilfred opened his eyes. "I haven't any mother," he told them. "She died when I was four years old. There's no one at home. It's the cook's day off."

"Oh-h!" said Ellie.

Chad tried to think what to do next. "We'll take you to our house. Our mother will take care of you."

Wilfred stretched his arms and then his legs. "I guess there are no bones broken," he said.

They waited a few minutes till some color came back

into his cheeks and he felt better. Then, one on each side of him, they helped him walk over the meadow to their house. They had him lie down on the couch in the living room. Ellie went to find Mother, who was in the garden working among the dahlias.

"What has happened?" she asked in a troubled voice, as they went into the house.

"Wilfred fell out of the old oak. His shirt is torn; and maybe he's hurt badly."

Mrs. Turner hastened her steps. Many times she had had to do for Chad and Ellie when they had accidents. She felt of his pulse. She had him stretch his legs and arms. She asked him where the pain was.

"I feel bad all over, but no special place."

"I'm glad there are no bones broken," Mother told him. "It was lucky that you fell on that soft grass. Just stay where you are for a little while and I think you'll be all right."

Meanwhile Ellie was making some hot chocolate. Wilfred gratefully lay back on the couch until Ellie came in with a cup of it. Then he surprised them all by sitting up and holding the cup himself.

He was very quiet as he drank the delicious chocolate. They wondered what he was thinking.

When he had finished and Ellie came to take the cup away, he said, "That was good! And you folks are very kind to do so much for me."

"We're glad we could help a little," Chad assured him.

"But it was a lot," Wilfred protested. "I've been mean to you. I don't know what I'd have done if you hadn't come over and helped me."

"Forget it," said Chad. "A feller would be awful mean if he wouldn't help when someone had bad luck like that."

Mother came in to find out how he was feeling. "Are you all right now?" she asked.

"Yes, I think I'm all right. I was terribly scared."

"Yes, of course."

She stayed around and watched to see whether there was any serious injury. "I'll send for a doctor at once if you feel any pain," she said.

Wilfred looked up into her face. "You're a nice kind lady," he said.

"Stay quiet on the couch for a while longer, till your father comes home. We'll watch for him."

In a little while Wilfred was looking at Chad's stamp collection. He soon had forgotten about his unpleasant experience, listening to Chad tell about the stamps of different countries.

Ellie brought him a glass of milk and a cooky.

"Thank you," he said politely. Then he added, as he

munched the cooky and drank the milk, "You folks are all very kind."

Seeing that he was not seriously injured, Ellie could not refrain from chiding him a little. "You shouldn't have tried to climb a tree with smooth leather shoes on. Didn't we tell you to wear rubber-soled shoes or go barefoot?"

"Yes, but I thought I knew better than anyone else."

"Oh!" sputtered Ellie. "Chad and I have learned a lot of things. We have learned what to do and what not to do."

Toward night they saw the cook come to the back door of the big house. "I must go," Wilfred said. "Thank you all very much for everything."

"Come over again," Mother invited him. "Come often."

Wilfred glanced around the room, not nearly so well furnished as his home. "This is a nice place," he said. "I'd like to come again."

He went out the front door and was starting down the steps when he stopped again and said, "Come over and climb the old oak tomorrow."

They watched him as he walked across the meadow. When he came to the sign, with its queer crooked letters, "No Treaspasing," they saw him pull it up and throw it on the ground.

Then, after he had gone on a short distance, he came back and picked it up and carried it off with him to his own place.

"Gee!" Chad exclaimed.

"He's not so contemptible after all," said Ellie.

11.   Thunder and Lightning

GRANDMOTHER HALE liked to sit on the front porch and
see what was going on around the place. She had seen
Wilfred when he put up the sign.

Now, for the next few days, she often glanced toward
the Turner house or the old oak and saw the three play-

ing together—Chad and Ellie and Wilfred.

"That's a good sight," she would say to herself. "Why some people want to put on airs and claim they are better than other folks, I could never understand. I'm glad those three have sense enough to have good times together."

One day Wilfred asked Chad and Ellie over to enjoy his television set. One day, he asked them to go riding, when the chauffeur was going to the city on an errand. And another day he invited them to go along to the beach. They went and had a good time.

Then there came a terribly hot day—hot and humid. The broadcaster giving the news over the radio said, "The temperature will reach ninety-five this afternoon. The humidity is now ninety."

"I wish I could hop into a cool lake," Chad exclaimed.

In the late afternoon a great stillness spread over the earth. Not a leaf moved. Not a twig swayed. The flowers drooped and withered.

"I wish it would rain," said Mother. "Then the flowers might revive. I wish there would be a little breeze."

She wiped the perspiration from her forehead and took up a palm-leaf fan. Ellie brought her a glass of ice water. Chad plugged in the electric fan and set it going.

"Thank you," Mother said heartily. "Those things help a lot."

The cat stretched out on the grass in the shade of the cherry tree in the back yard.

"I wish we had a car," said Chad. "I wish we could drive down to the beach."

The beach was only five miles away, but it took a long time to get there on foot.

"Why don't you wish for an airplane while you are about it?" Ellie asked. "Why don't you wish for a flying carpet? That would be the best. It would whisk us through the air in no time at all."

Mother went to the porch and looked up at the sky. "I think there's going to be a storm," she said. "Let's hope it will be a gentle rain that will cool the air and revive the flowers and the grass, but not a big storm that will do harm."

Late that afternoon it came. First, a little breeze sprang up. "Oh, how good to feel that blessed breeze," Mother said, as she sat on the porch writing a letter.

Dark clouds appeared in the western sky. The wind blew hard. The clouds scurried before the wind. There was thunder and lightning.

"Run upstairs and close the windows, Chad," Mother called.

"All right." And he ran up two steps at a time. He hurried from room to room closing windows.

"Ellie, please help me with the downstairs windows," Mother asked.

She herself hurried to the front room, while Ellie ran to the kitchen and tried to close the two windows. She had succeeded in shutting one when she heard a loud mew-ew.

"Oh, Frosty, come in out of the storm," she said, holding the screen door open.

Frosty scampered in and looked up at her gratefully, then went to her favorite corner and lay down.

After Ellie had finished the kitchen she hurried to the dining room. The wind was so strong by this time that it blew the curtains out into the room. It tipped over a vase of flowers standing on the table.

Ellie was still struggling with the west window when Chad came downstairs.

"Jeepers! What a wind!" he exclaimed.

He hurried over and tugged at the window to help Ellie, but even the two of them together couldn't get it down. The rain began to come in and sprinkled them with great drops.

A small branch of the apple tree came hurtling against the window screen and was held there by the wind.

Mother came to help; and all of them, pushing and pulling at the window finally closed it. "That will keep the storm out of the room, but no one knows what damage it will do outside," said Mother. "I hope our nice trees will not blow down."

The rain dashed against the window with a drumming sound. The wind roared and whistled around the house.

"I wish Grandmother Hale were not in her house all alone," said Mother.

"I'll go and bring her over here," Chad offered eagerly.

"Oh, no, you can't do that now. Even with your help she couldn't come across the road in all this storm."

By this time the rain was coming down in torrents. There was thunder and lightning every minute or two. They could scarcely see across the road. Chad stood by the window.

Suddenly he shouted, "There goes a limb of the old apple tree!"

Ellie ran to see it. "Oh, dear!" she moaned. "It had such good apples."

In another moment Chad exclaimed, "Gee, whillikens! There goes the elm tree, that big one up the road!" They watched it slowly fall over and lie across the road with a great crash.

"It was such a beautiful tree," Ellie sighed. "And what will the oriole do, the one that has its nest every spring in the top of it?"

"Oh, what if the old oak should blow down?" Chad said aloud what was in all their minds.

For a few minutes they all stood there wondering if the house would stand against such a fierce wind.

After a while it grew a bit lighter. When they could see across the meadow, Chad exclaimed, "There goes the old oak—the grand old oak."

But no. In a moment they saw that it had only bent over. It straightened again, as beautiful as ever.

"Oaks are strong as iron," said Mother. "It takes more than a storm like this to blow one over."

Then there came one more flash of lightning and a great crash of thunder. Ellie put her hands over her ears. A crackling, splitting sound came crashing all around them.

When it was over and the thunder had rolled away, Mother said, "That must have struck not far away."

"I'm glad it didn't strike our house," said Ellie. "I'm so glad we are all safe."

"I hope it didn't strike Grandmother Hale's house," said Mother.

"I'll go over and find out," said Chad. And he ran out of the house and across the road like a streak, though it was still raining a little.

He found Grandmother Hale in the front room of her home sitting in her favorite rocking chair.

"Are you all right?" he burst out. "We were worried about you, here all alone through the storm."

She smiled. "Sure, I'm all safe. I don't mind storms very much. I've been through a good many. But it was quite a storm, I'll admit."

"But you are all right?" he asked again.

"Of course I'm all right."

"Weren't you scared?"

"Scared? No; I like storms, especially when there is lots of thunder and lightning. Though I confess I was never in quite so rambunctious a one before. There was a crash a little while ago, somewhere in the back yard. I wonder what it was."

"I'll find out," said Chad. He ran to the back door. When he opened it something fell in. In the half light he couldn't see at first what it was.

In a moment he exclaimed, "A limb of a tree! A big limb!"

He managed to get through the door. There was a limb of the big cherry tree lying on the ground, its top having been hurled against the door.

Chad looked around the yard and garden. The flowers were lying flat on the ground. The bushes were bent over.

He ran back to Grandmother Hale. "A limb was blown off your big cherry tree!" he shouted.

"Oh, dear!" she said. "I remember when my father planted that tree. It bears delicious sweet cherries—almost white. I shall miss them."

"It's too bad," Chad said.

"But it might have been worse," was her quick remark. "I still have a house to live in. That stood the storm. It is built of oak, you know. It takes more than a storm like this to blow down a house made of oak."

Mother and Ellie came across the road. "We are so thankful you are safe," said Mother.

Ellie ran to the back door to see the big limb that had blown off.

"I wonder whether the old oak stood the storm all right," said Grandmother Hale.

Chad looked toward it. "I'll run over and find out," he said.

He ran across the road and over the wet grass.

12.   The Precious Find

WHEN Chad was a few rods away from the old oak, he saw something that made his heart skip a beat.

On the side of the trunk where the big limb had joined it, there was no longer any limb, big or little. There was only a long gash in the wood.

And on the ground under the tree there was the big limb stretched on the wet grass.

Chad stopped in his tracks. "Gee whillikens!" he exclaimed. "That big stroke of lightning!"

He stood there looking at the burnt streak that the lightning had made down the trunk of the great tree. It was near sunset. The sky in the west was beginning to show golden as the black storm clouds rolled away.

"If only that big stroke of lightning had hit something else," was Chad's thought. "Why did it have to spoil our tree?"

He ran back to Grandmother Hale's to tell the others. They were just coming out onto her porch after inspecting the damage in the yard.

"The old oak was struck by lightning!" he shouted as he came up the walk.

"Oh, dear!" exclaimed Ellie.

"I knew it struck somewhere near by," Grandmother Hale said. "Such a snapping and smashing!"

"What damage did it do?" Mother asked.

"It split the big limb off!" Chad told them.

"Our big limb?" Ellie asked, her lips trembling.

"Yes; one of those that held up the tree house."

"Oh, dear!" Ellie moaned.

"There's the rest of the tree," Mother reminded her.

"But we'll miss that big limb," said Ellie.

"It is a noble tree," said Grandmother Hale. "But oak trees do attract lightning. Maybe it is because their wood is so hard. Let's be glad the whole tree wasn't blown over by the wind."

Chad started back. Ellie followed. They scampered across the road and over the meadow, water splashing up on their legs as they stepped into little pools left by the rain.

Chad climbed up the tree. Just above the place where the big limb grew from the trunk of the tree, he found a hollow that had been covered before.

"Here's a new hollow!" he said. "The lightning tore off the bark that covered it."

Out of curiosity he kept feeling around inside the hollow place. All at once he called out, "Ellie, there's *something* in this hollow, something that doesn't feel like wood!"

"Can you get it out?" asked Ellie.

"I'm trying, but it is stuck tight in there. It feels like —why it feels very smooth and hard! It must be something made of metal."

"Oh, Chad, I'm coming up." She climbed up the rough trunk of the tree, just as she always did, but this time there was no big limb to sit on. She climbed to another branch and looked down at the opening of the hollow.

Chad kept feeling around inside. He couldn't see anything, even when he peered into the hollow.

"The opening to this hollow must have been quite big once," he said, "but the bark grew over it. And now the lightning has cut the bark off."

Twilight was creeping over the land. It was getting quite dark by this time in the depths of the tree.

"If I don't get it out soon, I'll have to go home and get the flashlight," said Chad.

"I'll go and get it," Ellie offered.

She slid down to the ground and was off like a deer. When she came back a few minutes later she had the flashlight in her hand. Chad took it and flashed it into the hollow.

"Jeepers! There's surely something in there—something that isn't wood!" he exclaimed.

He took his jackknife out of his pocket. A little cutting of the bark around the edges and he was able to put his hand in farther.

Ellie watched, breathless with excitement.

A few seconds later, Chad triumphantly brought something out of the hollow. It was a metal box about three inches wide and five inches long.

"Gee! Just the size Grandmother Hale said!" Chad shouted.

"But it doesn't look one bit like silver," said Ellie.

"See how dull and dark it is!"

"Maybe it's because it's been here so long. Let's go down."

As they dropped to the ground, a man came walking from the direction of the Mansfield house.

Now it happened that Wilfred and his father were away that week, having gone on a short vacation trip. This was the gardener, who had been left to care for the place.

"What are you kids doing here in Mr. Mansfield's tree?" he demanded in a stern voice.

Chad started to explain, but the man cut him short and said, "Let me have that box. No one has any right to things in that tree. They belong to Mr. Mansfield."

He took the box from Chad. "Off with you," he thundered.

Chad tried again to explain that they thought the box belonged to Grandmother Hale.

"You can prove that when he comes home," said the man. "I take no chances. I'll take this to the house and keep it till they come home. And see that you don't climb that tree any more."

"Maybe we'll never see that box again," Ellie moaned, as they started back across the meadow.

Before they had gone far they saw the Mansfield car

come into the yard. Wilfred, seeing Chad and Ellie, ran over to them.

Before he could even say Hello, Ellie spoke up, "Your gardener has taken the silver box away from us. We found it in the hollow where the lightning struck."

"What box? What hollow?" asked Wilfred.

It took some time to explain, but when Chad was through telling about it and Ellie had added some items, Wilfred said, "I'll get it back for you."

He ran after the man, who refused to give it up. "I will give it to no one but Mr. Mansfield himself," he declared.

Wilfred went along with him. "This little box was found in the oak tree after it was struck by lightning," the gardener explained. "Wilfred says it belongs to someone else, but it is my duty to guard your property, so I wouldn't give it up."

"Quite right," Mr. Mansfield told him. "Thank you."

When the man had walked away, Mr. Mansfield said, "Now tell me all about this matter, son."

"It probably belongs to Grandmother Hale. Come over to the old oak. Chad and Ellie will tell you."

Chad was a bit timid at first about claiming something that, after all, might belong to Wilfred's father as the owner of the land. But he gathered up his courage and spoke up bravely,

"Grandmother Hale left a box like that in the old oak about sixty years ago. We think that one must be hers. She wants it very much."

"Do you mean that a metal box left in the tree sixty years ago was still there?" asked Mr. Mansfield.

"That big stroke of lightning opened up the hollow," Ellie explained.

Mr. Mansfield looked at the big branch split off the tree. He examined the hollow Chad pointed out.

"Grandmother Hale says she put a silver box in a hollow in this tree when she was a little girl," Chad explained.

"Strange," said Mr. Mansfield. "But stranger things than that have happened. I'll go with you to see this lady."

The four of them went over to the house where Mother and Grandmother Hale were still sitting on the porch. Wilfred introduced his father, who said to Grandmother Hale, "Chad tells me that you left a silver box in that old oak a long time ago."

"Sixty years ago," she said.

"The stroke of lightning that split off that big limb brought this to light," he told her. He held out the box.

"Land sakes alive!" she exclaimed. "That's surely the box I left in a hollow in that tree one morning long ago, when we started west. It was bright and shiny then."

She took it in her hand and looked tenderly at it. Her eyes shone and her face lighted up with joy. "Oh, I'm so glad it has been found, so glad!" she exclaimed.

Mr. Mansfield looked at her thoughtfully. "Since I own the land and the oak tree now, I could claim anything found on it, but if it is yours, I want you to have it. Could you tell me what is in the box?"

"Yes; one thing was a picture of my brother who had died the year before. It was a small photograph. He was twelve years old. Besides that there was a letter, a sheet of paper folded to look like an envelope, that my mother had received a long time before. When she was packing to move, she was throwing away many things. I saw that letter and wanted it. I liked the pretty stamp on it. I had never seen one like it before. So I put those two things in the silver box, which was one of my treasures."

"Now we'll open the box," Mr. Mansfield said.

He found it was not easy to do, for the cover was held down tight by a clasp. They all watched breathlessly as he struggled with it.

Finally it came open. Mr. Mansfield's face showed astonishment.

"The box must be yours, Mrs. Hale," he said. "Look at this!"

They crowded around. In it was a photo of a boy about twelve years old—a handsome lad.

"My brother John!" Grandmother Hale exclaimed. Tears came to her eyes as she looked at it.

"I am so glad to have this picture of him again," she said. She looked at it long and lovingly.

"Thank you," she said.

"Thank Chad and Ellie," said Mr. Mansfield. "They were the ones who found it."

Next he reached into the box and took out a letter. It was about the size of the box and fitted into it nicely.

"It seems to be a letter," said Mr. Mansfield. "Like most of the letters in those olden times, it doesn't have an envelope, but the sheet of paper is folded to look like one."

"Is there a stamp on it?" Chad asked excitedly.

"Yes, there is a stamp on it." He held it up for all to see.

"Why, that's a postmaster stamp!" Chad shouted. "What is the date?"

Mr. Mansfield looked closely. "On the postmark there is the date August 21, but no year is given. If I may look inside at the letter itself, perhaps we may find the year."

"Yes, do look at the letter itself," said Grandmother Hale.

Mr. Mansfield unfolded the letter. "Yes, here it is at the top of the first page—August 21, 1846!"

"That is a rare postmaster stamp!" Chad shouted.

"Where was it mailed?" asked Grandmother Hale.

Chad looked at the postmark. "It is not all here," he reported. "Some of the letters are missing; but it looks like MILBU and at the bottom of the circle the letters MS."

"That means Millbury, Massachusetts," said Mr. Mansfield.

"It surely does," Chad agreed. "The postmaster there did put out a stamp of his own in that year 1846. There are only two or three known. It's a very rare stamp."

"Millbury, Massachusetts, did you say?" Grandmother Hale asked. "That letter must have come from my great-aunt. She lived in Millbury. My mother kept it all those years. Then I put it in the silver box and left it in the old oak."

"Hurrah!" Chad shouted.

Mother stood near all this time, wondering why they were all so excited. "Tell us just what a postmaster stamp is," she said to Mr. Mansfield.

"Surely," he replied. "Perhaps you all know that before 1847 there were no postage stamps on letters. People paid the postage when they received a letter or it was paid by the sender. Then the postmaster marked on the cover the amount of postage paid."

"I've seen many of those letters," said Grandmother Hale.

Mr. Mansfield went on, "Then there was a law passed that the Government would print postage stamps and people could buy them, just as we do now. But some postmasters didn't want to wait for the Government stamps, so they issued stamps of their own, even before 1847. Just a few postmasters did that. The postmaster at Millbury, Massachusetts, was one."

Grandmother Hale was too excited to talk much. Here was just what she had hoped would be found in the silver box, a rare stamp. She thought she might get as much as five hundred dollars for it, if she could find a buyer.

They all crowded around and looked at the rare stamp. It was of bluish paper, round in shape, with a picture of George Washington in the center, in black, and the words "Post Office" at the top and "Paid 5 cts" at the bottom, all the letters and lines in black.

Mother was happy because of Grandmother Hale's

good fortune, happy that her children had a part in finding it.

Mr. Mansfield said, "Would you sell the stamp, Mrs. Hale? I am a stamp collector myself. For years I have wished I could get one of those postmaster stamps."

"I might," she said quietly. "I wouldn't part with the picture of my brother for any amount of money, but the stamp is different. I might sell it."

Mr. Mansfield said quietly, "I will give you five thousand dollars for it."

Grandmother Hale was so astonished that she couldn't speak for a moment. Then she managed to say, "Thank you, sir. I will take your offer. Thank you heartily."

She was thinking how she could have a new roof put on the house and new paper on the walls and new steps in front and many other things. She said aloud, "I suspected lately that the stamp in that box was a rare one. Chad and my grandson told me about rare stamps, but I never imagined it would be worth as much as that."

"I'm getting a bargain," said Mr. Mansfield. "If you get a better offer, I'll match any bid you may get for that rare stamp."

"Thank you, sir," said Mrs. Hale again.

Then Mr. Mansfield said to Chad's mother, "Mrs.

Turner, I am most grateful for all you did for Wilfred when he fell out of the tree. And I'm grateful for what you and Chad and Ellie have done for him since. He was so unhappy when we first came here that it made him mean and boastful. Now he is a happy boy with such good friends."

"We'd like him to come over often and play with Chad and Ellie," said Mrs. Turner.

"One more thing," said Mr. Mansfield. "Perhaps you know that Wilfred had been dreading to start in this new school. He didn't want to go in our car with a chauffeur driving it, because he thought the boys would think him a sissy. And he didn't want to walk alone. I'd like to lend you one of our cars. If you could drive to school and Wilfred could ride along with his friends Chad and Ellie, it would solve a hard problem for me and I know it would make Wilfred happy."

"Hurrah!" shouted Chad. "We've been wishing for a car. And we'd surely like to have Wilfred ride with us."

"Thank you, oh, so much," said Mrs. Turner. "I can let the three of them off at their school, then I'll drive on to the high school. It will be wonderful."

"I'll send the car over in the morning," Mr. Mansfield said as he left. "It will be a small car—a sedan."

"All this is better than finding pirate treasure," said Grandmother Hale.

"Oh, boy! What good luck!" said Wilfred. In his heart he was thinking, "Once I was so mean I had no friends. And now just see all the good times I'll have, with Chad and Ellie."

"Come on, Ellie! Come on, Wilfred," said Chad. "Let's go over and climb the pirate oak."

As all three went racing across the meadow, Grandmother Hale said, "That's a good sight."

She picked up the picture of her brother and looked at it fondly.

The next morning the chauffeur brought over the car from the Mansfield garage. Mrs. Turner got in and took the wheel. She tried it up and down the road before letting the children in.

"It drives like a top," she said. "No more getting drenched with rain coming home from school."

"May we go to the beach today?" Ellie asked.

Mrs. Turner hesitated a moment, thinking of all the things she had planned to do that day.

"Yes, we'll go this very day," she said. "Get your bathing suits, then come and help me put up the lunch."

Chad and Ellie started off with a rush.

"Run home for your bathing suit and come back soon," she said to Wilfred.

Half an hour later, all three climbed happily into the car. Mother took her place at the wheel and off they drove for the broad white sands and the rolling tide.

Grandmother Hale waved her hand to them as they went past. That put something into Mother's mind. "Maybe she would go with us," she said.

She drew off to the side of the road and turned around. She drove back and stopped at Grandmother Hale's walk.

"Would you like to go to the beach with us?" Mother called.

"I go to the beach?" said Grandmother Hale. She hesitated only a moment. "I'd love it," she replied. "I've never seen the ocean."

A few minutes later the five of them were speeding along toward the broad white sands and the sparkling surf.

The End

Books by

HELEN FULLER ORTON

A LAD OF OLD WILLIAMSBURG
HOOF-BEATS OF FREEDOM
THE GOLD-LACED COAT
THE TREASURE IN THE LITTLE TRUNK
MYSTERY IN THE APPLE ORCHARD
MYSTERY OF THE HIDDEN BOOK
MYSTERY IN THE OLD RED BARN
MYSTERY OVER THE BRICK WALL
MYSTERY IN THE OLD CAVE
MYSTERY IN THE PIRATE OAK
MYSTERY UP THE WINDING STAIR
MYSTERY UP THE CHIMNEY
MYSTERY OF THE LOST LETTER
MYSTERY AT THE OLD PLACE
MYSTERY OF THE SECRET DRAWER
MYSTERY AT THE LITTLE RED SCHOOLHOUSE
THE SECRET OF THE ROSEWOOD BOX
GRANDMOTHER'S COOKY JAR